8-12

24.3

THE HOME RUN
KID RACES ON

**THE #1
SPORTS SERIES
FOR KIDS**

THE HOME RUN
KID RACES ON

Text by Stephanie Peters

LITTLE, BROWN AND COMPANY

NEW YORK / BOSTON

Little, Brown and Company

Hachette Book Group
237 Park Avenue, New York, NY 10017
www.lb-kids.com

www.mattchristopher.com

Little, Brown and Company is a division of Hachette Book Group, Inc. The Little, Brown name and logo are trademarks of Hachette Book Group, Inc.

First Edition: April 2010

The characters and events portrayed in this book are fictitious. Any similarity to real persons, living or dead, is coincidental and not intended by the author.

Matt Christopher® is a registered trademark of Matt Christopher Royalties, Inc.

Text written by Stephanie Peters

Library of Congress Cataloging-in-Publication Data
Christopher, Matt.
The home run kid races on / [text by Stephanie Peters]. — 1st ed.
p. cm. — (Matt Christopher the #1 sports series for kids)
ISBN 978-0-316-04481-3
[1. Sylvester improves his baseball skills while being coached by a man who bears a striking resemblance to baseball great Ty Cobb. 2. Baseball — Fiction.] I. Peters, Stephanie True.
II. Title.
PZ7.C458Hom 2010
[Fic] — dc22   2009017962

10 9 8 7 6 5 4 3 2 1

CWO

Printed in the United States of America

THE HOME RUN
KID RACES ON

1

Tell me again, why am I going to see some kid play baseball?" Duane Francis asked Sylvester Coddmyer III.

Sylvester, Duane, and a third boy, Snooky Malone, were riding along a winding bike path to a ball field a few towns away. Syl opened his mouth to answer, but Snooky beat him to it.

"Because he's a home run phenom," Snooky said, "just like Syl was after he met Mr. Baruth. Or *Babe Ruth*, as we think his real name is!"

Duane groaned. "Not that story again! I'm

1

telling you, Syl, that man was just some guy going around impersonating Babe Ruth."

"Actually," Syl said hurriedly, "I wanted to see this kid because our team will be playing his team, the Orioles, on Saturday. He plays third base, like you, Duane, so I thought it would be a good idea for you to check out your competition."

"But you *do* think Mr. Baruth could be there, right?" Snooky insisted. "That's the whole reason I'm coming!"

Sylvester glanced at his friend. "What do you mean?"

"My wildest dream is to have a paranormal experience—an experience you, my good friend Syl, have had not once, but *three* times!" Snooky explained. "I figure my best chance of having one is to stick close to you!"

Sylvester pedaled faster so he wouldn't see Duane's expression. He knew that Duane thought Snooky was an oddball. Not that Syl blamed him; he had trouble believing some of the weird stuff Snooky talked about, too. But then he would think about the strange and wonderful things that had happened in his baseball past…and suddenly, what Snooky believed didn't seem so far-fetched after all.

It had all started when Sylvester tried out for his first baseball team, the Hooper Redbirds. He'd always loved baseball, but he soon learned that loving a sport and being good at it were two very different things. Then he met a man named George Baruth.

Mr. Baruth gave Syl pointers on his stance, his grip, and other parts of his game. Almost immediately, Sylvester began to play better—*much* better, especially at the plate. After he met Mr. Baruth, he hit a home run in every game!

3

Word soon got out about the kid who only hit homers. Reporters showed up to interview him after his games. Photographers took his picture. A national magazine even offered him a lot of money for the rights to his story. They all asked the same question: How was he doing it?

"I just hit the ball squarely on the nose," Sylvester told them.

If they weren't satisfied with that reply, well, he couldn't help it. It was the best answer he could give because he wasn't completely sure himself how he was doing it!

Snooky, however, claimed to know where Sylvester's amazing abilities had come from. Snooky had a passion for astrology. He believed that the positions of the stars, the moon, the sun, and the planets affected people's lives on Earth.

"You're a Gemini," Snooky said, referring to the zodiac sign for people who were born at the end of May. "And right now, Geminis are very powerful. That's why you're hitting so well!"

Syl didn't buy all that astrology mumbo jumbo. He didn't believe Snooky when he said Geminis could "see into the beyond" either.

Not at first, anyway.

It was only much later, when Syl was knee-deep in an ongoing mystery, that he wondered if there wasn't something to what Snooky said after all.

George Baruth was a great help to Sylvester. But he was something of a puzzle, too. For one thing, no one but Syl had ever seen him, not even when Mr. Baruth was sitting in the crowded stands during games. For another, Syl always seemed to play his best when Mr. Baruth was there. By season's end, Syl couldn't help but wonder: Who *was* Mr. Baruth?

The mystery deepened the next year when Syl met a man named Cheeko. Like Mr. Baruth, Cheeko offered Syl suggestions on how to improve his game. Cheeko claimed to be friends with Mr. Baruth, so Sylvester trusted his advice.

Later on, however, he realized that Cheeko wasn't teaching him to play better, he was teaching him to play dirty. Sylvester refused to have anything to do with him after that—and the same afternoon, Cheeko vanished.

Syl made a startling discovery soon afterward, when he saw an old baseball card of the most famous ballplayer ever. The player was home run slugger George Herman "Babe" Ruth, and he looked *exactly* like Mr. Baruth!

Syl also found a card of an infamous pitcher named Eddie Cicotte. In 1919, Cicotte and seven of his teammates lost the

World Series on purpose in order to collect money from gamblers. When word of their plot got out, Cicotte and the other guilty players—the "Black Sox," as they were later called—were banned from professional baseball forever.

Amazingly, the pitcher was the spitting image of Cheeko!

The mystery didn't end there, either. Just this past summer, Syl met a man named Charlie Comet. Charlie taught Syl how to be a switch-hitter—that is, to bat right-handed or left-handed with equal skill. Switch-hitting came in quite handy, Syl soon discovered.

And he discovered something else, too. Charlie Comet looked just like a famous switch-hitter, Mickey Mantle!

That made it three times that Syl had been befriended and coached by men who looked *identical* to star baseball players. Duane suggested that the men were actors impersonating ballplayers who had died long ago, or that they just happened to look like those players.

Syl wasn't convinced. The only explanation he could come up with — as unlikely as it seemed — was that the men were *ghosts* of the famous players. Maybe, he thought, Snooky's belief that Syl could "see into the beyond" wasn't so far-fetched after all.

2

Duane and Snooky caught up to Sylvester on the bike path.

"I'm sorry, Snook, I just don't believe in that otherworldly stuff," Duane was saying. "And don't take this the wrong way, Syl, but why the heck would Babe Ruth bother with *you?*"

"You think I haven't asked myself that?" Syl retorted. "All I know is what he once told me — that he was just helping me realize my potential."

Snooky nodded knowingly. "And now you

think he's helping some other kid realize *his* potential, right?"

Sylvester didn't answer. But that was precisely what he'd been thinking.

"Or maybe," Duane offered, "this home run king is the real deal. You ever think of that possibility?"

"Sure," Syl said, "which is why it makes sense to check him out! So let's stop talking about Mr. Baruth and get to the field."

"Okay," Duane said, "but I'm doing it for the good of the Comets, not Snooky's cosmos!"

The boys arrived at the ball park just in time for the start of the Orioles-Jackdaws game.

Sylvester settled in the bleachers with his friends. Then, as casually as he could, he scanned the faces around him. But he didn't see Mr. Baruth. His gaze wandered back to the field—and suddenly, he spotted a lone figure standing just beyond the Orioles' dug-out. The man was tall, over six feet, and he was wearing an old-fashioned baseball cap.

Syl's heart leaped into his throat—and then just as quickly sank back down again.

It wasn't him. Mr. Baruth was stocky and had a round, moon-shaped face, a big nose, and a wide grin that lit up his whole face when he smiled. This man, on the other hand, appeared lean and muscular, and he was scowling. He also had prominent ears that stuck out on either side of his head. Those ears might have given him a comical look if not for that scowl.

Definitely not Mr. Baruth! Syl thought.

The sudden crack of bat meeting ball snapped his attention back to the field. Syl jumped up, certain he'd just missed the Orioles' phenom clobber a home run. It took him a moment to see that the batter had only made a base hit.

Of course the home run kid wasn't the batter, he berated himself. *Any coach worth his salt would have his top slugger batting cleanup, not leading off!*

The next Oriole batter struck out. Syl watched sympathetically as he trudged back to the dugout. He'd been there himself, plenty of times.

The third hitter fouled off two pitches and then tapped a short dribbler in the grass toward the first baseline. The pitcher nabbed the ball and threw to first for the out. The first baseman quickly relayed the ball to second, but that runner was safe.

Sylvester barely noticed. His attention was on the Oriole moving from the on-deck circle to the plate. The boy was the fourth batter in the lineup—the cleanup position.

"That's him," he muttered. "It's gotta be."

Sure enough, when the Oriole batter

stepped into the batter's box, everyone in the stands buzzed with excitement.

Syl craned his neck, trying to get a better look at the slugger's stance. How was he holding the bat? How were his feet placed? Was he a righty or a lefty? Sylvester hoped to see something—*anything*—that would tell him why this boy was such a good hitter.

But he saw nothing out of the ordinary. From the stands, the batter looked like any other player waiting for a good pitch to come his way.

That good pitch didn't come, however. The Jackdaws' hurler glanced at his coach and nodded. The catcher stood up and took a step to one side.

"Aw, man, he's going to walk him intentionally!" a fan in the stands complained. "Come on, it's only the first inning! Let him hit it!"

But the pitcher gave the Oriole a free ticket to first.

"You'll get one next time!" the same fan shouted.

Two innings later, however, when the home run kid got up a second time, he struck out.

The slugger didn't get up to bat again until the fifth inning. The Orioles were threatening with two runners on base and no outs. The Jackdaws' pitcher conferred with his coach—should he walk the Oriole, or pitch to him?

The coach must have signaled for him to pitch, perhaps hoping that the slugger would strike out or hit into a double play. If so, his hopes were dashed.

One pitch. One swing. And *boom!* The kid's bat connected squarely with the ball! It was a powerful hit, no doubt about it, but Syl thought the center fielder had a chance to catch it. He was wrong. The fielder misjudged where the ball was going to drop, and instead of landing in his glove, it fell on the far side of the fence.

"Holy cow!" Duane shouted.

The fans cheered as the runners jogged around the bases toward home. The slugger slapped hands with his teammates and smiled—a smile that widened as a man wearing a press badge snapped his photo.

An unexpected worm of jealousy wriggled in Syl's stomach. He swallowed hard and sat down.

Everyone else sat, too, except Snooky. "Man, oh man!" he cried in his high-pitched voice. "I've never seen a ball hit quite like that! Not even by you, Sylvester!"

Several people, including the home run kid and the newspaper photographer, turned to look at them.

"Pipe down, will you, Snooky?" Syl muttered, squirming.

The photographer studied Syl as if trying to place him. Then he snapped his fingers. "I know you! You're Sylvester Coddmyer the Third, the kid who only hit homers a while ago! I took your picture for the newspaper, remember?"

More spectators swiveled to stare. Syl hunched his shoulders, wishing that the bleachers beneath him would open up so he could escape.

The photographer didn't seem to notice Syl's discomfort. "You sure were the big story back then," he said with a chuckle. "So what's your story now? Still playing ball? Here to check out your number one competition?" He held up his camera. "How about a photo with you and the Orioles' slugger together?"

"No!" Sylvester hadn't meant to shout, but he couldn't take the man's questions, or the curious stares, any longer. He jumped up and thudded awkwardly down the bleachers.

"Syl! Wait!" Duane yelled.

But Sylvester didn't stop. He grabbed his bike and pedaled away from the ballpark as fast as his legs could take him.

3

The pavement beneath Sylvester's wheels twisted and turned, taking him past businesses, into and out of neighborhoods, and finally onto the bike path that went through an area of rolling hills and empty fields. After a while, he looked up and realized he didn't know where he was—or how he'd gotten there.

He stopped, wondering what he should do.

Just then, he heard a familiar sound. *Thock!* Somewhere nearby, someone had just hit a baseball; he was sure of it. But where?

Thock!

It's coming from up ahead! He pushed off toward the sound. He figured whoever was hitting those balls could give him directions back to town.

He rounded a corner and spotted a man standing in a tree-rimmed baseball field. There were bases marking the diamond, but the area looked as if it hadn't been in use for some time.

The field's condition didn't seem to bother the man, however. He hefted a wooden baseball bat above his shoulder, tossed a ball high in the air, and swung.

Thock!

Syl whistled softly. The man had an unusual grip, with his hands spread apart on the bat rather than close together, but his swing was powerful. The ball didn't soar into the sky. Instead, it sizzled straight into the trunk of a big oak tree. When it hit, birds flew from the branches above and leaves fluttered to the ground below.

Syl barely noticed, however. He was too busy staring at the man in open-mouthed amazement.

The second after he'd hit the ball, the man let go of his bat and took off at a full sprint. He rounded first base and continued to second. Then he dropped into a classic slide—feet first, bottom leg bent, top leg stretched out to touch the bag. The metal spikes on the soles of his shoes winked in the late afternoon sunlight and then disappeared in a cloud of dust.

Syl waited until the man hopped to his feet before speaking. "Boy, I wish I could move like that!"

The man whirled around, a look of surprise on his face. Sylvester blinked in sudden recognition. It was the man from the game, the one with the jug-handle ears!

"Hey, weren't you at the Orioles-Jackdaws..." Sylvester started to ask. But then he caught the man's expression and left the rest of his question unfinished.

The look of surprise hardened into the same angry scowl that the man had worn during the game. Sylvester dropped his eyes. As he did, he saw something on the man's pant leg that made him suck in his breath.

Spots of blood were mingling with the grass and dirt stains on the material. Syl realized that the man was wearing old-fashioned baseball pants—ones that had no padding whatsoever!

That slide must have scraped the skin clean off his leg! he thought.

"How you?" the man suddenly barked.

Syl started, looked up, and met a gaze so penetrating that he turned tongue-tied.

"S-s-sorry if I—I was wondering if you could point me back toward town?" he finally managed to say. "But I guess I could just retrace my steps." He started to turn his bike around, feeling foolish for not having thought of that sooner.

"Stop right there!" The man had a slight Southern accent, like the characters in a Civil War movie Syl had once seen. But it wasn't his accent that kept Syl rooted to the spot—it was his tone. He was a man who expected to be obeyed.

The man's eyes bored into Syl as if he were trying to see into Syl's mind.

"I know who you are," he said at last. "You're Sylvester Coddmyer the Third. You hit home runs."

Syl's mouth turned as dry as dust. "How do you know who I am?"

"How do I know who you are?" the man echoed Sylvester's question mockingly. "I've got ears, don't I?"

Sylvester remembered then how the

photographer had yelled his name and mentioned his past home run history. *The man must have overheard that back at the game. How else would he know who I am?*

Unless ... Syl felt a familiar tingling crawl up his spine. He eyed the man's old-fashioned baseball clothes. *Could he be another part of my mystery?*

"So you were some kind of home run hitter once, huh?" The man shrugged dismissively. "Can't say I'm too impressed by that. Any baboon can hit a home run. Now base hits, those are harder to knock out regularly. Bet a certain someone you know never told you that though, did he?"

Syl's heart gave a sudden bang in his chest. "A certain someone? Do you mean ... *Mr. Baruth?*"

4

Mr. Baruth? Yeah, I guess that's who I mean." The man gave a short laugh. "We're on opposite sides of the fence about home runs. He thinks they're everything. I don't."

Syl wrinkled his forehead in puzzlement. "You don't?" he asked. "Why not?"

"Home runs ruin batting averages, that's why," the man replied. "You swing for the fence every time, you'll strike out more often than you'll get a four-bagger. Or you'll get walked."

Syl remembered the Oriole slugger's first at-bats. "I guess that could be true, Mr...."

He paused, realizing that he didn't know the man's name.

"Teacy," the man said. "Mr. Teacy. And of course it's true. A player who can sprinkle hits around the field, he's worth something. He gets runners on base. He keeps the defense guessing. And he earns himself a high batting average and so keeps his place on the team." He shook his head. "A player who just hits home runs is like a singer who only performs one song. After a while, everyone knows just what tune they're going to hear. Bet Mr. Baruth never told you that."

Mr. Teacy picked up a baseball and tossed it to Syl. "Want to see one of my favorite hits?"

Syl nodded, intrigued.

"Then get on the mound and throw me a pitch," Mr. Teacy said.

"Okay," Syl replied, "but I'm not a pitcher."

"Just aim for the strike zone," Mr. Teacy

said as he retrieved his bat, "and I'll do the rest."

Mr. Teacy got into his stance in the batter's box. Syl took aim and threw. He didn't know what he expected to see, but he wasn't ready for what the man did.

Instead of swinging around in a wide arc, Mr. Teacy slid his right hand up the fat part of the bat, squared off, and knocked the ball to the ground so that it rolled toward third base.

"A bunt?" Syl said, surprised. "That's one of your favorite hits? But you can swing with so much power! Why would you bunt when you could send it over the fence?"

Mr. Teacy frowned. "Weren't you listening? Base hits, not homers! A well-placed bunt will get me on base. It'll advance runners, too, and catch the defense off guard. And that's a win-win-win situation." He held his bat out, barrel first, to Syl. "Let's see you do it."

Syl shook his head. "I'm no good at bunting," he admitted. "We usually work on regular hits during batting practice."

The man's lips flattened into a disapproving line. "Your coach must be a real lunkhead to ignore bunting!"

Sylvester swelled with anger then. He was very fond of his coach, Stan Corbin. He always encouraged his players to perform their best and to stay upbeat and positive, even when they didn't do as well as they had hoped. Whoever Mr. Teacy was, he had no right to criticize him!

"Coach Corbin doesn't ignore bunting," Syl said. "He just focuses on other things, that's all."

"Think what you want," Mr. Teacy said. "But if *he's* not showing you how to bunt, someone else better. And that someone" — he flicked his wrist, flipping the bat so the grip was now facing Syl—"is me."

Any doubt Sylvester had that Mr. Teacy was yet another piece of his baseball puzzle vanished in that instant. He reached for the bat, feeling that he was reaching toward his destiny.

To his surprise, Mr. Teacy didn't let go. "Not so fast," he said. "If I'm going to teach you, I want your promise that you'll give me everything you've got and that you'll follow my instructions to the letter."

Syl gripped the bat tighter, heart pounding. "When do we begin?"

Mr. Teacy allowed Sylvester to take the bat. "No time like now," he said. Then suddenly, he paused and looked in the direction of the bike path. "On second thought, meet me here tomorrow afternoon."

"What's the matter?" Sylvester turned to see what Mr. Teacy was looking at.

At that moment, Duane and Snooky appeared from around the bend. They looked tired and anxious. Then they spied Syl, and their faces brightened.

"Sylvester! There you are!" Duane cried.

"We've been searching everywhere for you!" Snooky added. "Why are you standing in an empty ball field?"

"Empty field?" Syl twisted around and saw that the field was, indeed, empty. Mr. Teacy had vanished.

"Hey," Duane said, "where'd you get that cool-looking bat?"

Syl's gaze dropped to the bat still in his hands. "This? I—uh, I found it lying here in the grass."

He told them how he'd gotten lost, but kept his meeting with Mr. Teacy to himself. He figured Duane wouldn't want to hear about another mysterious ballplayer. Snooky, on the other hand, would go on about how lucky Syl was to be in contact with another dimension. Syl wasn't in the mood for that just now. He needed time to sort out what had happened first. Maybe then he'd tell Snooky about Mr. Teacy.

Maybe.

"Thanks for coming to find me," he said instead. "You do know how to get home from here, right?"

"Sure!" Duane said. "I've biked here lots of times with my folks. Although," he added, scratching his head, "I don't remember this field being laid out like a baseball diamond. Weird."

Duane and Snooky waited for Sylvester to tuck the bat into his bike's carryall. Then they turned around to begin their journey home. As Syl pedaled away, he glanced at where the mysterious man had disappeared. *I'll be back tomorrow,* he promised himself.

5

It took the boys more than fifteen minutes to bike back to their hometown. There, they stopped for a drink at their local ballpark's water fountain. "I gotta take off," Duane said as he wiped his mouth. "See you here tomorrow, Syl."

Sylvester looked up from the fountain, confused. "Huh? Why?"

Duane rolled his eyes. "Duh! Earth to Syl! We have baseball practice after school, remember?"

"Jeepers, even I knew that!" Snooky put in.

"I just forgot for a second, that's all," Syl said, reddening. "I've got a lot on my mind."

"Like ghosts and home run kids?" Duane teased. Laughing at his own joke, he pedaled off.

The moment Duane was out of earshot, Snooky grabbed Syl's arm. "So did you see him? Did you?" he asked eagerly.

"See who?"

"Mr. Baruth!" Snooky said. "When I saw you staring at that old ball field and holding that strange bat, I couldn't help wondering—"

"No," Syl interrupted, shaking off Snooky's hand. "I didn't see Mr. Baruth."

"Oh." Snooky's disappointment was obvious. "Well, will you tell me if he or any other mysterious ballplayer gets in touch with you? Please?"

Sylvester scrubbed his face with his hands, suddenly weary. "Yeah, sure, whatever. I gotta get going. See you."

He knew he was being rude, but he couldn't help it. He didn't want to answer any more of Snooky's questions or see the hope in his eyes. So with a final wave, he turned his bike around and headed for home.

Delicious dinner smells greeted him when he walked into the kitchen. "Mmmm, I don't know what's in the oven," he said, sniffing appreciatively, "but I know it's making my stomach rumble!"

Mrs. Coddmyer smiled. "I made roast chicken and vegetables," she told him. "There's French bread warming, too. Everything will be done in about fifteen minutes."

"I'll set the table," Syl said.

He was putting the final fork in place when Mr. Coddmyer returned home. He took a deep whiff of the kitchen air and grinned. "I love that you cook such wonderful meals!"

"And I love that you clean up when we're

done eating our wonderful meals," Syl's mother replied as she placed the dishes of food on the table.

While they were eating, Mr. Coddmyer told them a funny story about a coworker whose young daughter had surprised him by packing a lunch in his briefcase. "All day, he smelled something weird in his cubicle," Mr. Coddmyer said. "But it wasn't until the afternoon that he opened his case and found the tuna sandwich she'd put in there! Pee-yew!"

Sylvester cracked up, imagining how awful the smell must have been. Mrs. Coddmyer laughed, too. Then she mentioned a meeting she'd had with some neighbors to organize a neighborhood yard sale.

"The money we raise will go toward a big block party this summer." She turned to Syl. "I'd like your help sometime this week. There's a lot of old junk in our attic and basement that we can donate, but we have to sort through it all first."

"I can help anytime except tomorrow afternoon," Syl said. "I have baseball practice."

He hesitated then. He knew he should tell them about Mr. Teacy and ask for permission to work with him at the old field the next day. But he didn't. They would have asked a lot of questions about who Mr. Teacy was and why they were playing at such an out-of-the-way place. He had no answers to those questions. So instead, he asked if he could get in some extra practice the following afternoon.

"I want to work on my bunting," he added.

His parents agreed. "Just take your cell phone with you," his mother said, "and call me when you leave the ball field so I know you're on your way home."

So the next morning Syl left for school

with his baseball gear — glove, cap, cleats, and uniform — strapped to his bike's carryall. He made sure he had Mr. Teacy's bat, too.

Classes seemed to drag by at an impossibly slow pace that day. Even his favorite period, lunch, took forever to get through. But at last, the final bell sounded.

He found an empty bathroom and changed into his purple and white Comets jersey and baseball pants. Then he hurried outside to the bike rack. He was just about to unlock his bike when he heard Snooky Malone call his name.

"Oh, no," he groaned.

"Thought you could ditch me, huh?" Snooky crowed when he reached Syl's side.

"Snooky," Syl said impatiently, "you can't follow me around all the time!"

"Why not?" Snooky protested.

"Because it's creepy, that's why! Besides,

I'm not going anywhere interesting today, just to baseball practice. And if I don't leave now, I'm going to be late!" With that, he hopped on his bike and pedaled off, turning a deaf ear to Snooky's shouts.

Ten minutes later, he arrived at the town baseball field.

"Yo, Syl! How's it going, man?"

Sylvester looked up to see Trent Sturgis approaching. Behind Trent was Jim Cowley. Duane arrived a moment later, as did Coach Corbin and several other players. Sylvester greeted them all, and then stuck his cap on his head and put on his glove. After a moment's hesitation, he grabbed Mr. Teacy's bat from his carrier.

Coach Corbin lifted his eyebrows when he saw the bat. "Trading aluminum for wood?"

"Only if it's okay," Syl said.

The coach took the bat and examined it closely. "I'm sorry, Syl," he said. "Your bat isn't regulation size for our league." He handed it back.

Syl had forgotten about the league rules concerning bats. "I'll leave it with my stuff on the bench," he promised.

When they ran out on the diamond, Coach Corbin ran his players through some warm-ups. Then he announced the first drill.

"We'll start with some batting and infield practice," he said. "When I call your name and position, head out to the field. On the mound, Bongo Daley. Eddie Exton, you're at catcher. First base, A. C. Compton. Second base, Jim Cowley. Shortstop, Trent Sturgis. Third base, Duane Francis. Everyone else, find a bat."

Sylvester glanced at Mr. Teacy's bat. He pictured how the man had used it to bunt the ball down the third baseline and wished that he could give it a try himself.

I can see it now, he thought, closing his eyes and smiling.

The Comets are facing the Orioles. It's the final inning of a five-to-five tie ball game. The Orioles' third baseman has slugged two homers today, good for three of his team's runs. I've been just as strong at the plate, however, clocking three hits deep into the outfield already. Now I'm at bat again, so the Oriole fielders move back.

But I surprise them all. Instead of clobbering the ball, I round to the pitcher and knock it into the dirt! The ball snakes through the grass toward third. The Oriole slugger scrambles forward to get it, but he's too late! I'm standing on first, and the crowd is going wild.

"Syl? Syl!"

Sylvester opened his eyes to find his teammates looking at him with amusement.

"When you're done daydreaming," one of them said, "the coach wants you to take your turn at bat."

6

Sylvester flushed from his neck to his scalp. He found his favorite aluminum bat in the pile and hurried to the batter's box.

"Try for a grounder," Coach Corbin suggested.

Syl knew the coach expected him to do a full swing. But his imaginary bunt was still so fresh in his mind that he decided to try that hit instead. So when Bongo's pitch came, he squared off toward the mound and shifted his grip so his hands were spread wide apart on the bat.

Everything went just as smoothly as it had

in his daydream — until the ball hit the bat. *Tink!* Instead of landing on the ground in the shallow infield, the ball popped straight up. Eddie Exton lunged to his feet and caught it easily.

"Let's stick to full swings for now, Syl," Coach Corbin called. "We'll bunt later, if there's time. Take another cut."

"Yes, sir," Syl said sheepishly. Determined to make good this time, he swung from his heels on Bongo's next pitch. It was a solid blast, and he grinned as the ball soared into right field and hit the fence for what would have easily been a double in a game situation. But his grin faded a second later.

"*In*field practice, Sylvester, remember?" Coach Corbin said dryly.

"Sorry, coach," Syl muttered. "I — I'll go get it."

"Please do."

Syl jogged to the back fence to search for

the ball. Suddenly, he heard someone call his name.

"Coddmyer, how come you're not using my bat?"

Syl spun around to find Mr. Teacy standing behind the fence. "What're you doing here?"

"I go where I like," Mr. Teacy said. "So, the bat?"

Syl told him about the league's equipment regulations.

Mr. Teacy snorted. "Regulations! A player should be able to use whatever wood he wants, if you ask me. He should also be allowed to practice whatever kind of hit he wants to," he went on, giving Syl a significant look.

"Coach Corbin said we'd work on bunting later," Syl said defensively.

"*If* there was time," Mr. Teacy corrected. He made a face. "Well, forget him. We'll work on it later, right?"

Syl hesitated. He *did* want to practice bunting with Mr. Teacy. Yet somehow, he felt it would be disloyal to Coach Corbin if he did.

Mr. Teacy seemed to guess what he was thinking. "No harm in extra practice, is there?"

Syl couldn't disagree with that. "I'll be at the old field after practice," he said. "But now I've got to find the ball."

"You mean this?" Mr. Teacy produced the missing ball from behind his back.

"Thanks," Syl said, reaching for it.

To his consternation, Mr. Teacy didn't hand it over. Instead, he threw it in the dirt at Syl's feet. "See you later," he said as he turned on his heel and stalked away.

Syl watched him for a moment before picking up the ball. When he straightened, Mr. Teacy was gone.

Just like the others, Syl thought as he hustled back to home plate, *except he's not as nice. Heck, even Cheeko made me laugh!*

Coach Corbin continued infield and batting practice for a while longer, spending time with several players on their stances and swings. Then he called everyone back to the bench to explain the next drill.

"Infielders, back to your positions. And in the outfield, let's have Steve Crenshaw at right, Sylvester Coddmyer at center, and Kirk Anderson at left."

"What about us, Coach?" a boy named Mike asked.

"You and the others are going to be my runners," the coach said. "We're playing fungo-rungo."

"Huh?" Mike looked confused. "What's that?"

"A fungo is when the coach tosses the ball up in the air and hits it," Steve informed him.

"I know what a fungo is," Mike said. "But what's a rungo?"

"That's when you *run* to first after I hit the ball," Coach Corbin said. "Or overrun it to beat the throw. Then if you're safe, on my next toss, you *go* — as in steal second. And then third, if you can."

"I get it," Mike said with a laugh. "Fungo-rungo!" He jumped to his feet. "What're we waiting for? Let's go-go!"

Syl enjoyed the game of fungo-rungo. He made a few good catches in the outfield and once even relayed the ball to Eddie Exton for an out at home plate. Then, when it was his turn to run, he made it safely to first on the coach's fungo into left field. He advanced to second on a line drive hit at the pitcher that Bongo ducked. Rod Piper in center field picked up the ball, but the runner, Kirk, beat his throw to first.

"Glove at the ready next time, Bongo,"

Coach Corbin called. "Fielders, try for a double play! Runners, you know what to do!"

Syl glanced over at Kirk and saw he was taking a big lead off first. Syl inched off his bag, too, so a moment later when the ball left the coach's hand, he was already a few steps closer to third.

Thock! Coach Corbin blasted a high fly ball into center field. Syl watched as Rod lifted his glove and faded back. It should have been an easy catch. In fact, Syl was on his way back to second to tag up when he heard a yell.

"Rod dropped the ball!" Kirk bellowed. "Go!"

Syl wheeled around and raced toward third. He glanced up and saw Duane with his glove raised and ready.

Rod must have decided to try to get me out

instead of Kirk, Syl realized. *Well, that's not going to happen!* He picked up speed.

All of a sudden, Duane ran off the base. Rod's throw was wild!

"Hit the dirt, Syl!" Coach Corbin called.

Syl wasn't very good at sliding, but he didn't want to let the coach down. So he dove toward third, arms stretched out in front of him. Even before he heard his teammates' shouts, he knew he was in trouble — at that same moment, Duane leaped back toward the bag, his hard rubber spikes on an intercept course with Syl's hand!

7

Syl squeezed his eyes shut, waiting for Duane to spike him. Then—

"Oof!" The breath rushed out of his body as Duane fell on top of him instead.

The coach was at their side in a flash. "Are either of you hurt?"

"I'm okay," Duane gasped as Jim pulled him to his feet.

"Syl? How about you?"

Syl rolled onto his back with a groan. "I think Duane got me out," he said with a weak grin. He sat up to the sound of laughter.

Coach Corbin checked him over to be sure

he wasn't seriously injured. "Your ribs may be sore tomorrow," he said, helping him up. "But other than that, you should be fine."

Then he called the team together. "This seems like a good time to talk about sliding," he said. "Who can tell me what Syl did wrong?"

With an apologetic look at Syl, Trent raised his hand to answer. "He went in headfirst."

"Why is that bad?" Coach Corbin prodded.

Trent replied, "Because if you go headfirst, you could get hurt really badly. The base player could accidentally kick you in the head or stomp on your neck or hit you in the face with his glove or grind his spikes into your hand or—"

The coach cut him off with a nod. "I think you've made your point, Trent. Thank you." Then turning to the rest of the team, he said, "Diving slides do put you at much greater risk for serious head and neck injury." He smiled at Syl. "So no more belly whoppers, okay?"

Syl nodded.

Coach Corbin checked his watch. "We don't have much time left," he said. "Let's use it to focus on sliding. Everyone except Jim, Syl, and Eddie line up behind home plate. On my mark, take off for first base, touch the bag, keep running, and slide into second."

He pointed to Jim, Syl, and Eddie. "Grab your gloves and head to your positions. Eddie and I will take turns throwing the ball from home to second so you, Jim, can practice making tags. Remember to sweep your glove up and away from the runner after the tag so he can't knock the ball free."

Jim gave him a thumbs-up sign and hurried onto the field.

"What about me, Coach?" Syl asked.

"Back up Jim in case he misses a catch," Coach Corbin said.

Syl was dismayed at being sent to shag balls, but he tried not to let it show. *Coach probably just wants to give me a chance to recover from Duane falling on me,* he reasoned as he found his glove. He touched his rib cage and winced. *I guess it is a little sensitive.*

Still, standing in the field behind second base waiting for Jim to misjudge a throw was boring. Syl watched his teammates slide into second, but after a few minutes, that got tiresome, too. When a bright yellow butterfly flitted into his line of vision, he allowed his gaze — and his mind — to wander after it.

Why can't butterflies fly in a straight line, like birds? I wonder what it feels like to be cooped up in a chrysalis? I've seen yellow, orange, and blue butterflies but never purple —

"Heads up, Syl!"

The ball had gotten past Jim. It got past Syl, too. He scrambled after it, plucking it from the grass with his bare hand. If it had been in a game, A.C., the runner, would have made it safely to second standing up.

"Sorry, Jim," Syl said sheepishly. He got into his ready stance, determined to pay better attention from then on.

A few minutes later, the coach called him in to take a turn at sliding. Syl tossed his glove into the dugout and ran to the plate. He crouched, waiting for the signal.

"Go!" Coach Corbin barked.

Syl took off as fast as he could run. Dust flew up in a thick cloud behind him as he toed first base and pushed off toward second. As he did, a sudden gust of wind blew the dust cloud over him. Temporarily blinded by the grit, he had no idea how close he was to Jim or the bag.

I better hit the dirt, just in case!

He dropped down into a bent-leg slide.

Unfortunately, he started too far away and ground to a halt with inches between his foot and the base.

Jim caught the throw and stepped on the bag for the out. Then he grinned, touched Syl lightly with his glove, and sang out, "Ting!" as if he'd tapped a crystal goblet with a spoon.

Laughter filled Syl's ears. He joined in to cover his embarrassment.

"This is why we're doing the drill, folks," Coach Corbin said. "If you don't practice the slide, you won't be able to do it properly during a game. And that could cost your team."

Fortunately for Syl, practice ended shortly after that. The coach reminded everyone that the tee-ball league had the field for the rest of the week, so he wouldn't see them until the game on Saturday.

"Try to get some extra practice on your own, if you can," he added. "We're playing the Orioles."

Syl and Duane exchanged glances. "They're tough," Duane said. "At least, one of them is—a kid who only hits homers."

The coach caught Syl's eye and grinned. "Well, we know what it's like to have one of those on the team, don't we? But even if we don't slug out big hits all the time," he added, "we've got a good team. Right?"

The boys cheered and then broke off, laughing and talking, into small groups.

Syl found an open spot on the bench and changed his spikes for his sneakers. He was dog-tired from practice and wanted nothing more than to bike home and relax. But Mr. Teacy was waiting for him. So, with a deep sigh, he made his way to his bike.

"Syl, wait up!" Trent hurried over to him. "Do you have your cell phone?" When Syl nodded, Trent grinned. "Excellent! Call your mom and see if you can come over to my house. I got a sick new four-player video game. Jim and Duane already got the okay to come and play it, so now we just need you."

Syl hesitated, thinking.

He hadn't actually *promised* Mr. Teacy he'd meet him today, had he? And there was no practice tomorrow or the next day, which left two entire afternoons open for bunting practice. Wouldn't it make more sense to go then, when there'd be lots of time, instead of now, when he was due home for dinner in an hour? Not to mention the fact that he was so tired he wouldn't be in his best form today!

No, he finally decided, *I'll wait until tomorrow*.

"Just give me a minute to call my mom," Syl told Trent. "If it's okay with her, then I'm game to play *your* game!"

8

Sylvester had a great time playing Trent's new video game. In fact, he didn't give Mr. Teacy another thought until the next morning.

"Mom," he said over breakfast, "would it be okay if I went to the ball field right after school? I never did get in any bunting practice yesterday."

He had expected his mother to agree, but to his surprise, she shook her head. "Not today, Syl," she said. "I need your help getting ready for the yard sale, remember?"

Syl groaned. He'd totally forgotten about the sale.

Mrs. Coddmyer laughed at his reaction. "Tell you what," she said. "You give me an hour right after school this afternoon and tomorrow, and after that, you can have until dinnertime for baseball. Deal?"

Syl knew it would be useless to argue. So instead of pedaling to the old ball field when school let out that afternoon, he pedaled home. There he found his mother puttering in the garage among boxes, bags, and bins filled with junk.

"What *is* all this stuff?" He poked around inside the nearest bin and pulled out an old camera. "Would someone seriously pay money for this?"

Mrs. Coddmyer glanced up. "That's my old point-and-shoot camera. I took a lot of pictures of you with that thing."

Sylvester examined the camera more closely. "Hey, I think there's still some film in it."

"Let me see." His mother checked it and nodded. "You're right. There are one or two exposures left on the roll." She handed the camera back to Syl. "Put that somewhere safe. There's a shop downtown that still develops film. If the film hasn't been ruined from being in the attic, maybe we'll add some new photos to our stash."

Sylvester laid the camera on the garage steps. As he did, he had a sudden idea.

I could bring this camera with me today and sneak a photo of Mr. Teacy! Then I'd have proof that he is real!

With that thought in mind, he turned back to his mother. "Say, Mom, could I use up the film before we get it developed? It seems like a big waste not to finish the roll."

Mrs. Coddmyer shrugged. "Sure, why not?"

"I'll drop the film off at the shop after I finish bunting practice," Syl added as he tucked the camera into his gear bag. Then he returned to helping his mother sort through the boxes. He found many other "treasures," including a bin of his favorite T-shirts.

"Why do we have these still?" he asked his mother, holding up a bright blue shirt he'd worn constantly when he was five years old.

She smiled. "I'm going to turn those into a patchwork quilt for you someday. If you dig a little deeper, you'll find your Redbirds and Hawks team shirts in there, too."

Syl imagined sleeping under a quilt made from his old shirts and smiled, touched by his mother's plan. Then he pawed through the bin until he found the Redbirds jersey. He stared at it, remembering all the great games he'd played while wearing it.

That season was all thanks to Mr. Baruth,

he thought. He wondered if he'd ever see the mysterious man again. He hoped so.

He'd just finished refolding the last of the shirts when he caught a glimpse of the time. "Oh, no!" he cried. "Mom, can I be done for today? I need to get to the ball field!"

She made a shooing motion with her hands. "Go, go! But be home by six for supper, okay?"

"You got it, Mom!"

Twenty minutes and a furious bike ride later, he reached the old ball field.

"Mr. Teacy?" he called. "Mr. Teacy, are you here?"

For a long minute, there was no reply. Then Mr. Teacy stepped out from behind the oak tree.

"Where were you?" he thundered.

Syl tried to explain, but Mr. Teacy cut him off.

"Save it," he said angrily. "We've lost too

much time already." He narrowed his eyes and stared at Syl. "I assume you're prepared to give me everything you've got from here on out?"

Syl bit his lip and nodded.

Mr. Teacy grunted. "Grab my bat and go to home plate for bunting practice."

Syl turned to get Mr. Teacy's bat from the back of his bike. He had just freed it when suddenly, he heard a new voice.

"You're going to need a pitcher if you're going to be bunting."

Syl wheeled around in disbelief. "Mr. Baruth?" he cried, overjoyed.

"It's me, Sylvester Coddmyer the Third," the moon-faced man replied with a wide grin.

"I can't believe it's you!" Syl said.

"I can't either." Mr. Teacy strode across the field, eyes blazing. "What're you doing here, Baruth?"

"I'm here for the same reason you are," Mr. Baruth replied evenly. "To help Syl—if he wants me to, that is."

"What makes you think it's up to him?" Mr. Teacy demanded. "I'm running the show here!"

"Is that so?" Mr. Baruth's congenial manner suddenly vanished. He took a step toward Mr. Teacy, his meaty hands balled into fists.

"Hold on!" Syl intervened. He turned to Mr. Teacy. "Doesn't it make sense for him to pitch to me while you show me how to bunt?"

Mr. Teacy looked from Syl to Mr. Baruth and back again. "Fine," he said shortly. Then he jabbed a finger at the other man. "You do what I tell you, though, or you're out of here!"

Syl held his breath. Would Mr. Baruth put up with Mr. Teacy talking to him like that?

Fortunately, Mr. Baruth relaxed his hands, picked up a ball, and walked to the mound. Only then did Syl let his breath out.

Mr. Teacy jerked his head at Syl, directing him toward the plate. Once there, he launched into a lecture about bunting.

"Bunts work best when there's an element of surprise, so don't ever let on that you're going to do one," he said. "Most common is the sacrifice bunt, where the batter's main goal is to advance a runner. Usually, the batter gets out—that's why it's called a sacrifice. Name some other bunts."

Syl thought hard, chewing on his bottom lip. But he couldn't come up with any answers.

"That coach of yours teach you *anything*?" Mr. Teacy blew out an impatient breath and then rattled off the names of different bunts: "Safety squeeze. Suicide squeeze. Push bunt. Drag bunt. Any of these ringing a bell?"

Syl shook his head miserably.

"Give me the bat," Mr. Teacy ordered. "We'll focus on the drag bunt. It's my favorite because nine times out of ten, it'll go for a base hit—if it's done right, of course."

He drew a batter's box in the dirt by home plate and stepped inside with his feet near the top of the rectangle. "Assume your normal stance, but stand closer to the pitcher. When he commits to his pitch, square off, slide your hands apart, and because you're a righty, point the barrel at first. Aim to knock the ball down the third baseline. After the hit, run like a demon is chasing you."

With that, Mr. Teacy handed the bat back to Syl. Then he threw a ball to Mr. Baruth on the mound and called, "On my signal."

Mr. Baruth waved to show he understood.

Mr. Teacy backed away from the plate. "You ready?"

"Wait!" Syl's mind was whirling with all the

information Mr. Teacy had thrown at him. "I'm not sure I remember—"

"The only way you're going to get this is to do it!" Mr. Teacy shouted. "So get into your batting stance!"

Syl snapped his mouth shut, stepped to the front of the batter's box, and hefted Mr. Teacy's bat over his right shoulder. His heart hammered so hard in his chest he thought it would burst.

"Pitch!" Mr. Teacy suddenly yelled.

Mr. Baruth coiled into his windup and threw. Syl turned forward, slid his hands down the bat, and held the barrel out toward the incoming ball.

Clunk!

"Ow!" Instead of the ball hitting the wood, it hit Syl's thumb!

9

Syl dropped the bat and danced around, shaking his injured hand and grimacing in pain.

Mr. Teacy snatched the bat from the ground. "Don't you even know how to hold the bat during a bunt? Your fingers and thumb pinch the barrel top and bottom, they don't wrap around it!"

He shoved the bat back into Syl's hands. "But I guess you won't forget that again, will you? Now get back into the batter's box and try again."

Syl felt like a fool. Of course Coach

Corbin had taught him the proper grip for a bunt; he'd just forgotten. But he doubted Mr. Teacy would believe him. The man clearly didn't think the coach knew anything!

"You all right, Syl?" Mr. Baruth called from the mound.

"He's fine." Mr. Teacy threw the ball back to the pitcher. "Get in your stance," he growled at Syl.

Syl did, although a big part of him wanted to hop on his bike and pedal away. Then he glanced at Mr. Baruth, who gave him a thumbs-up and a smile. He smiled back and shouldered the bat.

Mr. Teacy leaned forward, hands on his knees. "Pitch!"

In came the ball. This time when Syl stepped around, his hands were in the proper bunting grip. *Thock!* He hit the ball with the bat this time—and cringed the moment he did. Instead of sending the ball bounding through the grass, he'd popped it into the air, just like he had in practice the day before.

Mr. Teacy darted forward and caught it. Glaring at Syl, he opened his mouth to speak.

But this time, it was Syl who cut him off. "I know!" he shouted. "I hit the ball with the top part of the barrel, not the bottom! That's why it went up instead of down! I'm sorry, okay?"

Syl was certain Mr. Teacy would tear into him for his outburst. Instead, Mr. Teacy gave a slow smile. "So, there's a fire in that belly of yours after all! Good. Just be sure to direct that energy at the other team. Ready to go again?"

Sylvester felt his anger fizzle until all that remained was determination. He lifted the bat over his shoulder, bent into his stance, and aimed a steely-eyed stare at Mr. Baruth. "I'm ready," he said.

And to his amazement, he *was* ready. Mr. Baruth hurled pitch after pitch. Syl hit several drag bunts in a row with success. When he did mishit one, he corrected his mistakes and hit the next few right. After half an hour, he was breathing hard—and Mr. Teacy was nodding with great satisfaction.

"Not bad, Coddmyer," he said. "Go get a drink and then come back so we can move on to the next lesson."

"Next lesson?" Syl looked at him with surprise. "What else is there for me to learn?"

Mr. Teacy's good humor vanished. "There is always something to be learned!" he said. "Sure, your bunting has improved, but you haven't even done the most important part!"

Syl took a long drink from his water bottle. "And what's that?"

Mr. Teacy rolled his eyes. "Beating the throw to first base! If you can't do that, every bunt will be a sacrifice, won't it?" He threw his hands in the air and went to talk to Mr. Baruth.

Sylvester knelt down to put his water bottle back into his bag. As he did, he saw the old camera he'd stashed there earlier. His heart started pounding. He glanced up at the two ballplayers. They were standing together on the mound. Neither was looking in his direction.

Now's my chance, Syl thought. He pulled the camera from the bag. *I can get both of them in the same photo. Just one shot, and I'll have proof of their existence!*

Slowly, so as not to attract attention, he lifted the camera to his eye and centered the men in the viewfinder. With one push of a button, he snapped the photo.

Click!

The sound was like a gunshot to his ears. He dropped the camera into his bag, certain the men must have heard its click. Mr. Teacy didn't seem to notice anything. Mr. Baruth, on the other hand, shifted his gaze to stare at Syl.

Syl's mouth turned dry. *Did he see me take the picture? What will he say — or do?*

Mr. Baruth muttered something to Mr. Teacy. Mr. Teacy turned. He didn't look at Syl, however, but at something behind him.

Sylvester spun around just as a biker barreled around the corner. It was Snooky Malone!

"You!" Syl cried. "What are *you* doing here?"

10

Snooky dropped his bike and hurried toward Syl. "I know you don't want me to shadow you," he said. "In fact, I almost couldn't because I didn't know where you'd gone. I called your house, and your mom said you were at bunting practice. But the tee-ball league has the field. Then I remembered this place."

"What made you think I'd come here?" Syl wanted to know.

Snooky shot Syl a confident look. "You had a peculiar expression on your face when standing in this old ball field the other day.

It's an expression I've seen before. You've had another encounter from the beyond, haven't you?" He kicked at a weed. "Just my luck to get here too late to see the ghost."

Syl knew then that Mr. Teacy and Mr. Baruth had vanished. He gritted his teeth in frustration. He'd hoped to spend more time with Mr. Baruth. But unless Snooky left, that wasn't going to happen. With a sigh, he zipped up his bag. "There's nothing to see here, Snooky," he said.

Snooky didn't look convinced. "Nothing to see here *now*," he amended. He held his hands out toward the field as if testing the air. "But I sense a cosmic energy here. If we stick around, I bet your ghost will return."

"Bet anything you like," Syl said. "I'm leaving."

Snooky's shoulders slumped. "No point in my staying then," he said, his voice thick with disappointment. "You're the key that unlocks the door to the other side. I could knock until my knuckles are raw. Without you, that door just won't open."

Syl bit his lip. He hated seeing his friend upset, but what could he do? He didn't control who saw the ghosts.

Or did he? He blinked. If the photo he'd taken came out, he could show it to Snooky. It wouldn't be the same as seeing the real thing, but it was better than nothing. And he owed his friend at least that much. After all, Snooky was the only one of his buddies who truly believed in his mysterious ballplayers.

I'll drop off the film on the way home, he decided, *and pick it up later tonight. If the photo is good, I'll call Snooky to come see it.* He laughed to himself. *Who knows? Maybe I'll call the newspapers, too!*

"Cheer up, Snooky," he said, slinging a leg over his bike. "Just because you didn't see anything here doesn't mean you won't see something someday."

Sylvester and Snooky rode back to town together but parted at the ballpark. Once Syl was sure Snooky was gone, he veered toward the local shopping mall to find the camera store.

He was so busy looking at store signs that he didn't notice that his bike wasn't riding smoothly. When he finally did, he groaned. His back tire was flat!

He pulled into the mall parking lot to consider his options. He carried a patch kit for just such emergencies, so he could fix the tire. Or he could call his mother to come get him. He decided to call. But when he looked for his phone inside his gear bag, he couldn't find it. He groaned again, remembering that he'd left it at home, plugged into its charger.

Patch kit it is! He removed his gear bag

from the back of the bike to make the job easier. He'd just started working when he heard a familiar voice.

"Ew, pew, what's that smell? Must be a Codd-*fish!*"

It was his archenemy, Duke Farrell. Duke was a pitcher; every time they met on the diamond, he did his best to make Syl look like a loser at the plate. But Syl had always let his bat do the talking and turned the tables so that it was Duke who ended up with egg on his face.

Syl glanced back and saw that Duke's sidekick, Steve Button, was with him. "Leave me alone, you guys," he growled.

"Let's play a game first," Duke said. "This is one of my favorites. I call it keep-away!" He grabbed Syl's gear bag.

"Hey, give it back!" Sylvester shouted, standing up.

Duke waggled his finger. "Not until you

play!" He flung the bag over Syl's head into Steve's waiting hands.

Syl tried to snatch it, with no success. Frustration boiled up inside him. "I don't have time for this! Give me my bag!"

Steve hefted the bag over his head. "Make me!"

"You asked for it!" Syl said and then barreled straight at Steve.

"Ooof!" Steve fell onto his backside. The bag flew out of his hands and landed right in front of an oncoming pickup truck!

Crunch!

As the truck rolled over the bag, the driver's head snapped up. Steve scrambled to his feet and took off with Duke right behind him. The woman leaned out her window and stared at the lump behind her tire, a look of horror on her face. "What *is* that?"

"It is—was—my baseball stuff," Syl replied sadly.

While the woman parked the pickup, Syl retrieved his belongings. He sat on the curb and examined the contents one by one. His glove and ball were fine, but his water bottle had been crushed to smithereens. So had the camera.

The woman put her hand to her mouth. "Oh, no, look what I did!"

"It wasn't your fault," Syl protested. "It was those other boys. They threw the bag in your way."

But the woman shook her head. "You don't understand," she said. "I was texting when I pulled in here. I should have been paying attention to my driving, but I wasn't." She sat down next to him and put her head in her hands. "What if that had been a *child*?"

Sylvester patted her back awkwardly. "It wasn't, though."

After a few minutes, the woman took a deep breath and stood up. "I'll replace your things, I promise," she said. "But for now, let me give you a lift home."

Syl nodded. "Can I use your phone to call my mom first?"

Fifteen minutes later, the truck pulled into the Coddmyers driveway. Mrs. Coddmyer hurried out.

"I'm fine, Mom," Syl said before she could pepper him with questions.

The woman and his mother talked while Syl unloaded his bike and his gear. He gave the broken camera one last look before dropping it into the trash can.

Sorry, Snooky, he thought. *I tried.*

After the woman left, Mrs. Coddmyer showed Syl a check she had given her. "She insisted on buying us a new camera," she said. "I told her it wasn't necessary, that your phone can take pictures and that the camera hadn't been used in years anyway. But she felt so bad, she wouldn't take no for an answer."

It wasn't until Sylvester was in bed that night that something his mother had said came back to him. "Your phone can take pictures." He sat up.

My phone can *take pictures!* he thought excitedly. *Maybe I'll be able to show Snooky photos of Mr. Baruth and Mr. Teacy after all!*

Then he realized his plan had a flaw. It was only one problem, but it was major: He had no way of knowing if Mr. Teacy or Mr. Baruth would show up at the field again the next day. They'd vanished that afternoon before he could ask.

All I can do is go back to that field tomorrow, he decided, *and hope!*

Getting to the old ball field alone the following day wasn't easy, however. First, he had to persuade his mom to let him go right after school. "I'll help with the yard sale tonight, I promise!" Then, Trent cornered him after school to coax him into playing the video game with Duane and Jim again.

"Uh, I have a lot of homework and I might have to help my mom," Syl said. "So I have to go home."

Trent didn't press him further, but then Duane caught him strapping Mr. Teacy's bat onto the back of his bike.

"What's that for?" Duane asked curiously. "Trent said you were heading home."

"I am," Syl replied. "I have the bat because, uh... because I hoped Coach Corbin would check it out, see if it's regulation so I can use it during practices and games!"

"Didn't he do that already, when you first showed it to him?"

"I, uh, yeah, I'd forgotten about that," Syl answered. "So now I'm bringing it back home. See you!"

Before Duane could ask any more questions, Syl jumped onto his bike and pedaled off. He only went a short distance, however, before looking back to see if Duane was still there. He wasn't, so Syl switched his direction from home to the bike path. He stopped only once, to change into his baseball pants.

Fifteen minutes later, he arrived at the old ball field. To his disappointment, neither Mr. Teacy nor Mr. Baruth was there. He sat down, opened his bag, and pulled out his cell phone to check the battery. The power bar indicated that the phone was fully charged. He took a few test photos of his feet. They came out fine, so he dropped the phone back into his pack.

"How are you?"

Syl started. There was Mr. Teacy, leaning against the oak tree, a spot Syl knew had been empty just moments before.

"I'm fine, Mr. Teacy!" he replied. "And ready for some more practice. We were going to work on beating the throw to first today, right? Hmm, guess I better switch into my baseball shoes for that, huh? I've got them right here in my bag, so I'll just get 'em and put 'em on!"

Stop babbling, he berated himself, *and just do it!*

Heart racing, he reached into his bag and flipped the cover of the phone open. The tiny screen glowed.

"What's taking you so long?" Mr. Teacy barked.

Syl grabbed one of his baseball shoes to use as cover. With shaking hands, he raised the phone out of the pack, centered Mr. Teacy in the middle of the screen, moved his thumb over the buttons —

And the screen went black.

11

You deaf or something?" Mr. Teacy said. "I asked, what's taking you so long?"

Sylvester stared at the dark screen in dismay. Then he closed the phone and dropped it back into his bag.

"Sorry, I had a knot I couldn't get undone," he answered. As quickly as he could, he switched his sneakers for his spikes. "Say, isn't Mr. Baruth going to be here today?"

"No," Mr. Teacy said shortly. "He had someplace else he had to be."

Syl was disappointed but tried not to show it.

"Let's hope you're faster on the base paths than you are at untying knots," Mr. Teacy grumbled when Syl joined him at home plate. "Show me what you've got."

"What do you mean?" Syl asked.

"I mean *run!*" Mr. Teacy cried.

Startled, Syl took off down the base path like a horse that'd been stung by a bee.

"You call that running?" Mr. Teacy mocked. "I've seen ducks waddle faster!"

Sylvester picked up his pace, slowing only when he reached first.

Mr. Teacy stormed up to him. "Didn't I tell you to give me everything you've got?"

Syl nodded dumbly.

"Then why'd you slow down? You do that in a game and you'll be picked off. Get back to home plate. And this time, round first and slide into second."

Sylvester hesitated, remembering how

poorly he'd slid during practice with the Comets.

"Well?" Mr. Teacy thundered.

Syl hurried back to home plate and got into a runner's stance.

"On my mark," Mr. Teacy said. "Ready? *Go!*"

Syl pushed off and began to run. To his surprise, Mr. Teacy did too—except he didn't run *with* Sylvester so much as *after* him!

"Go!" he screamed. "Faster! Move those legs! Dig it out! Faster, boy!"

Maybe it was Mr. Teacy's yells, or maybe it was the adrenaline that suddenly shot through Syl's veins, but whatever the reason, Syl did run faster. In fact, he practically flew across the dirt toward first base. He touched the bag and kept going. Then, when he judged he was close enough to second, he bent his left leg beneath him, dropped, and slid toward the base with his right leg outstretched.

To his relief, unlike in practice, his foot reached its target. In fact, his whole right leg crossed the bag so that when he stopped moving, he was half resting on the base.

Mr. Teacy stood over him, looking appalled. "*That's* your slide?" he said.

Syl took a deep breath and sat up. "That's my slide," he replied defensively, his face turning red. "What was wrong with it?"

"You overshot the mark by a mile. Your hands were in the dirt when you slid," Mr. Teacy said, ticking each point off as he talked. "Your right leg was ramrod straight. And now you're just sitting there like a bump on a log!" He shook his head in a gesture of pure disgust.

Sylvester flushed an even deeper red.

"Come on," Mr. Teacy said, "I'll walk you through it." He started back to the plate without waiting to see if Syl was following.

And Syl almost didn't follow. What made him return to the plate was something Mr. Baruth had taught him long ago: It was better to try and fail than to quit.

So with a determined squaring of his shoulders, Syl went back to home.

"You got the running part down that time anyway," Mr. Teacy said. "But you dropped into the slide way too late. Follow me."

With Syl at his heels, Mr. Teacy circled the base paths toward second. He stopped at the spot where Syl had begun his slide. "Not here," he said, backing up several paces. "Here. Nine to ten feet from the base."

He waved for Syl to come next to him. "Show me how you begin the slide."

Syl bent his left leg so that his foot was behind his right knee. Dropping down to the ground from this position was awkward, however, so he braced himself with his hands.

"Stop!" Mr. Teacy barked.

Syl stared at him, bewildered. "What'd I do wrong *now?*"

12

"You put your hands down, that's what you did wrong," Mr. Teacy answered grimly. "You do that when you're sliding and you'll snap your wrist in two or jam and scrape your fingers! Ever try catching, throwing, or batting with a broken wrist or bloody, bent fingers? Not so easy. Lift your hands and cup those fingers like you're holding an egg in each palm."

Syl did as he was told. Now he was sitting in the dirt with one leg bent beneath him, the other out in front, and his arms held high. "Like this?" he asked, wobbling as he tried to balance on his hip.

Mr. Teacy blew out an exasperated breath. "You slide on your backside, not your leg! The seat of your pants should be filthy when we're through! Now raise your right foot higher. Bend that right knee when you hit the bag! You keep it straight like you did before and you'll destroy the joint, guaranteed."

Once more, Syl made adjustments to his position. Mr. Teacy circled him a few times and then nodded. "Better. Now get up."

Syl lowered his hands, intending to push himself up.

"No!" Mr. Teacy roared. "Use your *legs* to pop you up, like you would in a real slide!"

Syl tried his best to get to a standing position by just using his leg muscles. But he couldn't.

"Just get up," Mr. Teacy finally said. "You

think you can put everything together? Do a slide that will get you safe on base?"

"I think so," Syl said, but his voice lacked confidence, even to his own ears.

Mr. Teacy snorted. "Well, we'll see. Back to home. I'll watch from here."

Syl hurried to home plate. At Mr. Teacy's signal, he took off running. To make sure he went as fast as he could, he pictured Mr. Teacy chasing him. The tactic worked magic. He chewed up the base paths faster than he could have imagined possible.

When he reached the point for his slide, he bent his left leg, dropped onto his backside, held his hands high with cupped fingers, and reached out with his right foot for the bag. His momentum was just right, carrying him across the dirt and past where Mr. Teacy was standing. His aim was right, too; his toe tagged the bag but didn't sail over it. When it touched, he let his knee give a little to absorb the impact. Best of all, he managed to pop up to a standing position — without using his hands.

"I did it!" he crowed.

"You did it *once*," Mr. Teacy corrected. "Do it again."

Sylvester's second slide went just as well as his first — and so did the one after that, and all those that followed. After his tenth trip down the base paths, sliding felt so natural it was as if he'd known how to do it all along.

But when he said as much, Mr. Teacy looked at him like he was crazy. "Anyone can slide into an empty base," he scoffed. "How will you do when you face a player protecting the bag? Or when you're trying to steal?"

Sylvester's happiness evaporated. "Guess I still have a lot to learn," he mumbled.

To his surprise, Mr. Teacy smiled. "That's the first smart thing I've heard you say all day," he said. "The ballplayer who thinks he knows everything is the ballplayer who finds himself sitting on the bench." He folded his arms across his chest. "You were lousy at bunting. We fixed that. You were lousy at sliding. We fixed that. Are you lousy at stealing, too?"

"I don't know," Syl mumbled.

Mr. Teacy snorted again. "That's closer to a yes than a no," he said. "So tell me, if you're a runner planning to steal, what part of the pitcher's body should you watch?"

"His shoulders or his head," Syl replied confidently, "because he'd turn to look at me."

"You're only half-right," Mr. Teacy said. "An inexperienced right-handed pitcher will turn his head and shoulders in order to look at first base. If he's going to throw to first for a pickoff, his head and shoulders will rotate even farther in that direction. But if he's going to pitch, he'll turn back—and *bam!*"

He slapped his fist into his palm. "That's when you take off!

"But," he continued, "if you have a pitcher who knows what he's doing, you watch his *feet*. If he's a righty, he'll lift his front foot before he pitches." He demonstrated by raising his own foot. "When it goes up, you go! But," he added, "if the back heel comes up, get back to the bag *fast* because chances are, he's about to pivot and throw to his first baseman."

"That makes sense," Sylvester said, nodding. "But what if the pitcher is a lefty?"

"A southpaw is already facing first base so he doesn't have to pivot. Watch just his front foot. He'll raise it and then step toward home plate if he's pitching—"

"—or toward first if he's going for the pickoff, right?" Syl finished.

Mr. Teacy nodded.

Syl looked at the empty mound. "Too bad

Mr. Baruth isn't here to pitch. Then I could work on bunting, sliding, and stealing."

Mr. Teacy's good humor ebbed away. "You don't need him to do that. Get on the mound and pitch it to me. Field the ball, pitch again, and then cover second."

Wondering what Mr. Teacy had in mind, Sylvester found a ball and trotted to the mound.

Mr. Teacy strode to the batter's box. He hefted his bat and glared at Syl.

"Pitch!"

13

Sylvester reared back and threw. Mr. Teacy laid down a bunt that dribbled toward the mound. Syl scooped it up and turned to see Mr. Teacy standing on first. He took a big lead off the bag and signaled for Syl to pitch again.

Syl went into a windup. As his front foot lifted, he heard Mr. Teacy take off for second. He got rid of the ball as quickly as he could and rushed to cover second. Unsure of what he should do next, Syl crouched in a pantomime of a catch.

He looked up to see Mr. Teacy barreling at

him like a runaway train. His brain screamed for him to run off the base. But he steeled himself as Mr. Teacy hit the dirt in a slide.

But it wasn't a normal slide. Instead of keeping his outstretched leg low and near the bag, Mr. Teacy aimed it high — and suddenly Syl was looking at the business end of some very sharp metal spikes!

"Yow!" He leaped aside just in the nick of time. "Are you crazy?" he shouted at Mr. Teacy. "You almost gored me!"

Mr. Teacy gave a soft laugh as he dusted off his pants. "Yeah, but I made the steal, didn't I?" He adjusted his cap and added, "Now it's your turn."

"What? No way!" Syl shook his head vehemently.

Mr. Teacy took a step toward him. "You said you'd follow my instructions without question," he reminded Syl.

Syl stood his ground, refusing to be

intimidated. "Yeah? Well, guess what? I *am* going to ask some questions, but they're not about your instructions!" he yelled. "Like, who are you, really? Who is Mr. Baruth? Why did you choose me and not someone else? Why only me?"

The questions came out in a rush of emotion. He hadn't meant to ask them that way, but now he put his hands on his hips, waiting to see if Mr. Teacy would answer.

Mr. Teacy fixed him with a humorless smile. "What makes you so sure you're the only one?"

Syl recoiled as if he'd been slapped. "You mean... I'm not?"

Mr. Teacy didn't answer, just continued to smile.

Tears suddenly pricked Syl's eyes. He dropped his gaze to his feet. "That Oriole," he whispered. "Mr. Baruth has been coaching him on how to hit homers, hasn't he?"

Mr. Teacy still didn't reply.

"*Hasn't he?*" Anger mixed with betrayal caused Syl's voice to crack. When Mr. Teacy still didn't speak, he jerked his head up, ready to demand an answer.

But Mr. Teacy had vanished.

"Syl? Syl! Are you okay?"

Sylvester whirled around to see Duane, Trent, and Jim biking toward him at break-neck speed. Anxiety was etched across their faces.

"We heard you shouting!" Trent said breathlessly. "What's the matter?"

"Nothing," Syl mumbled. "I just— nothing."

"What're you doing out here, anyway?" Jim asked. "I thought you were doing home-work or helping your mom."

"Well, I thought you guys were playing video games," Syl countered.

Trent rolled his eyes. "My mom made us

quit for the day. Said it was too nice outside to be holed up inside. We were going to play a little pitch, hit, and catch at our ball field, but that tee-ball tournament is still going on."

"Then I remembered this place from the other day," Duane put in, "so we decided to play here instead. We would have come sooner if we'd known you were here already." He gave Syl a questioning look then.

Syl looked away. "Well, since we're all here, why don't we play some ball? Come on, Duane, you're on my side. I'll pitch first."

The others readily agreed, and so for the rest of the afternoon the four boys took turns batting, catching, and running the bases. Syl laughed and joked along with them.

But deep inside, threads of anger and jealousy were slowly twining into a knot. With every passing moment, that knot was growing, and at its center was Mr. Baruth.

14

Despite being tired from hours of baseball, Syl slept poorly that night. Luckily, the next day was Saturday, so he got to sleep in. Still, when he finally did rise, he was out of sorts. Not even his favorite game-day breakfast of bagels and cream cheese lightened his mood.

"You better work yourself out of your snit before you hit the diamond," his mother advised after he'd snapped at her one time too many. "I don't think Coach Corbin would appreciate that kind of attitude!"

The mention of Coach Corbin only made

him more irritable. *If the coach had taken the time to teach me how to bunt and slide properly, then Mr. Teacy wouldn't have shown up. And I would have never figured out that Mr. Baruth was coaching that other kid!*

Syl knew he was being unreasonable. Coach Corbin had never shirked his responsibilities to his players. And Mr. Baruth had never said Syl was his only protégé.

But why did he have to pick someone on a team we play? Syl wondered angrily.

He and his parents arrived at the ball field soon after breakfast.

"Here we are," his father said as he parked the car. Sylvester grabbed his glove and his cap and got out, slamming the door with a bang.

"He's become a 'tweenager,'" he heard his mother say.

"Lord help us!" his father replied with a laugh.

Ha, ha, thought Syl.

Many of the Orioles and Comets were already at the diamond warming up. Syl joined his teammates and caught a throw from Trent. He turned and hurled the ball with all his might to Eddie Exton. It landed with a loud pop in Eddie's mitt.

"Whoa, Syl!" Eddie called, freeing his hand and shaking it. "Save it for the game, man!"

"Sorry," Syl muttered. He toned it down for the rest of warm-ups.

The Comets were the home team, so Sylvester jogged out to his spot in center field. He had one thing on his mind: getting back at Mr. Baruth by robbing the slugger of any home run he might attempt to hit.

If I have to leap the fence to make the catch, I will! he thought, pounding his fist into his glove.

Bongo Daley took a few practice pitches

and then signaled that he was ready. The game began.

In the Orioles-Jackdaws game a few days earlier, the first Oriole batter had hit a single. This time, against the Comets, he rapped out a grounder that took a funny hop over the path between first and second base. That hop gave the Oriole time to reach second. The next batter popped a fly ball to Duane at third for the first out. The runner on second wisely stayed put.

One out turned to two when the third batter fouled off two pitches and then missed a third. That brought up the home run kid.

"Back up!" Syl screamed to Steve and Kirk as he backpedaled into deep center field. *And if you see me coming, get out of my way!* he added silently.

He squinted at the slugger, watching his every move. He wasn't trying to guess where he'd hit it, however. He wanted to see if the

Oriole glanced into the stands. If he did, that's where Mr. Baruth would be.

But the Oriole seemed more concerned with staring down Bongo than looking for his mysterious coach. Bongo took Eddie's signal, nodded, coiled back, and threw.

Zip! went the ball.

Swish! went the bat.

Pop! went Eddie's mitt.

"Strike one!" shouted the umpire.

"Told you so," said someone behind Sylvester. "Players who try to clobber the ball for homers whiff on more pitches than they hit."

Syl didn't even have to turn around to know who was there. "Yeah, you told me, Mr. Teacy," he said. "You told me a whole lot. Now I'm going to tell you: leave me alone. I've got a game to play."

Mr. Teacy laughed softly. "I'll leave you alone," he said, "but I'm not going to leave.

Not until I see you put my lessons to work, that is. So the sooner you show me what you've learned, the sooner I'll be gone."

Syl didn't have time to say anything in return because at that moment, the slugger put what Mr. Baruth had taught *him* into practice.

"Heads up, Syl!" Kirk yelled. "It's all yours!"

15

Sylvester whipped his gloved hand up into the air and kept his eyes glued to the ball soaring through the blue sky. He moved a few steps to his right, positioned himself directly under the ball, and waited for it to fall into his glove's pocket for the out.

To his astonishment, the ball didn't drop into his glove. Instead, it seemed to veer away just before he caught it.

"What the—?" He spun around, scrabbling in the grass. He finally picked up the ball and threw to the cutoff man. But he was too late. The Oriole had already rounded third on his way to an in-the-park, two-run homer.

"Syl, what the heck happened?" Kirk bellowed from left field.

Syl shook his head. He couldn't believe he'd missed it either. In fact, he was certain he should have caught it. He replayed the ball's trajectory in his mind. It was coming down on a line right to his glove—until suddenly, it wasn't.

No, Syl fumed, slapping his empty glove against his thigh, *that miss wasn't my fault. Something or someone made that ball change course. And I bet I know who it was.*

He narrowed his eyes and scanned the visitors' stands. Then he looked at the people in the hometown bleachers. He saw Mr. Teacy leaning against the fence. Search as he might, though, he didn't see Mr. Baruth anywhere.

Of course, I didn't see him at the Jackdaws-

Orioles game either, he reminded himself. *That doesn't prove he wasn't there — or that he's not here right now!*

He was so busy thinking about Mr. Baruth that he didn't realize Bongo had retired the Orioles until Steve called for him to hustle in for their turn at bat.

Syl was batting cleanup, so there was no guarantee he would get to the plate that inning. Jim, the lead-off hitter, started the Comets off strong by ripping a line drive past the second baseman, good for a single.

Syl applauded with his teammates, happy for his friend. Then he picked up a bat and began swinging it. It appeared as if he'd get his turn after all, and when he did, he wanted to be ready.

Eddie was up next. He had a powerful swing that sometimes yielded hits but more often led to him striking out. This time, he managed to send the ball to shallow right field. He made it to first and chose to stop. Jim, however, rounded second and continued on to third.

"Slide!" the third base coach yelled. *"Slide!"*

Jim hit the dirt. The throw came in low and hard. A flurry of dust blocked Syl's view. *Is Jim safe or out?*

The umpire fanned his arms to either side. "Safe!"

Syl and the rest of the Comets let out a whoop. Coach Corbin applauded madly, grinning ear to ear. Syl grinned, too, in part because he was proud of Jim—but also because the third baseman, the Orioles' slugger, had lost out that time.

Kirk came to the plate with runners at first and third and no outs. When the pitch came, he swung from his heels, clearly hoping to homer and put his team ahead. Instead, he hit a blooper. The shortstop faded back and caught it easily.

"Okay, Syl," Coach Corbin said in a low voice. "We could use some power now."

Sylvester nodded and walked toward the batter's box. As he did, he saw a movement behind the bench.

It was Mr. Teacy. He was holding his bat, but not in a normal batting grip. His hands were spread wide, with the fingers of his right pinching the fat part of the bat.

Drag bunt, he mouthed to Syl.

Syl hesitated. He glanced back at Coach Corbin for confirmation that he was to hit away. The coach was busy talking with the next batter.

Syl looked into the outfield and saw that the players there had backed up, just as he had done for the Oriole slugger. He shot Mr. Teacy a brief nod and stepped into the box.

The pitcher leaned in and took the signal. He began his windup.

Wait for it, Syl thought, his heart racing. *And . . . now!*

The pitcher reared back. With a swift motion, Syl squared off, slipped his hands apart, and aimed the end of the bat's barrel toward first.

"Oh no!" he heard the catcher cry. Then the bat drilled the ball to the ground between home and third, and all Syl heard after that was the sound of his own breath as he high-tailed it for first.

He made it!

"Nice bunt, Syl!" Rod, the first base coach, said with excitement. "You totally fooled the infield, especially their third baseman! He practically fell over his feet trying to get to the ball in time!"

"That so?" Syl said, laughing. "Wish I'd seen it!"

"It's just too bad Jim didn't know it was coming," Rod said, "or he might have made it home. Instead, he looked kind of confused. I think he was hoping you'd clobber the ball. Oh, well. He didn't have to run, did he? And now the bases are loaded, so we're in good shape!"

16

Syl was sorry to have confused Jim but saw with satisfaction that his bunt had rattled the Orioles' pitcher even more. A quick conversation with his catcher and his coach calmed him down. He caught A.C. looking on two pitches and then got him to swing on the third for the Comets' second out. That brought up Duane.

"Come on, Duane, you can do it!" Syl yelled. "Don't let us die out here!"

Duane very nearly *did* leave them stranded. He fouled off three pitches to right field before clocking the fourth one fair. The ball flew over the first baseman's outstretched glove and bounced along the fence. The right fielder scrambled to pick it up. When he did get it in his hand, however, he seemed uncertain where to throw it.

Finally, with his teammates screaming at him, he hurled it as hard as he could toward the catcher. But his throw was so wild that both Jim and Eddie scored easily. Syl was safe at third and Duane was standing up at first!

Tie ball game, and Syl was in place for the go-ahead run!

Unfortunately, the next batter was Bongo. Bongo was a terrific pitcher, but he was lousy at the plate. He took three cuts and missed each one to end the Comets' turn at bat.

Syl hurried to get his glove and then hustled to center field. He and the other outfielders threw the ball around a few times. Then the umpire yelled, "Play ball!" and the second inning began.

Nothing much happened that inning, or the two after that, however. Syl and his teammates returned to the field for the fifth inning with the score still 2–2. It didn't stay that way for long, because Bongo suddenly seemed tired. He gave up three hits in a row to load the bases!

When the fourth batter strode to the plate, the Orioles' fans cheered and the Comets' fans groaned. It was the home run slugger.

Coach Corbin jogged to the mound to give Bongo a quick pep talk. Syl, meanwhile, gave himself one as he backed up. "Go ahead, hit it to me," he growled. "Your streak ends now!"

The Oriole did hit it to center field — deep, *deep* center field! Syl faded back until he collided with the fence. But he didn't give up. As the ball fell to earth, he jumped, stretching his right arm as high as he could.

He might have caught the ball, too, except

just as it neared his glove, he felt a sharp sting on his bare skin. Pain shot down his arm, making him involuntarily jerk it down.

Plop!

Instead of nestling in his webbing, the ball dropped over the fence for a grand slam.

"No!" Syl cried, hurling his glove to the ground. He looked at his arm and saw a small, red welt—and a yellow-and-black insect buzzing away. "A *bee sting?* Are you *kidding* me?" He turned in circles, searching for...what? A bee's nest? Or someone to blame the sting on?

Of course, he found neither. *Just rotten luck*, he finally told himself. But he didn't believe it, not even for a minute. Two sure-fire catches muffed by strange coincidences? Not likely!

With that hit, Coach Corbin decided that it was time to replace Bongo with their other pitcher, Burk Riley. Bongo slumped off the field and sat on the bench, head down, while Burk, with his fresh arm, quickly retired the side.

"Okay, Comets," Coach Corbin called, clapping his hands, "let's get it back!"

Eddie Exton was the first at bat. He looked two balls into the catcher's glove and then took a ball to his shoulder on a wild pitch. He tossed his bat aside and jogged down to first base. That brought up Kirk. Last time up, Kirk had flied out to the shortstop. This time, he flied out to deep right field! Fortunately, Eddie was a fast runner, and he made it to second after tagging up.

Now Syl stepped into the batter's box. He wondered if the fielders would back up, as they had last time. They didn't, but he saw a few of them shift their feet, as if unsure what to expect.

Syl decided to hit away rather than try another bunt. So when the Oriole pitcher gave him one he liked, he swung. *Pow!* The ball blasted between the third baseman and the shortstop and bounded into left field. Syl made it safely to first and turned in time to see Eddie, unbelievably, beat the throw to third!

"Woo-hoo!" Syl cheered. "Way to dig it out, Eddie!"

"Now it's your turn to dig it out," came a familiar voice. Syl sneaked a look over his shoulder and saw Mr. Teacy standing behind Rod, the first base coach. "Take a big lead and get ready to steal."

Syl swallowed hard. "Are you sure?"

"Am I sure of what?" Rod asked.

"Nothing," Syl said, shifting off the bag to stand several paces into the base path.

"Remember—" Mr. Teacy began.

"—to watch the pitcher's feet," Syl finished in a whisper.

The Oriole pitcher stretched his arms over

his head and brought them down in front, turning to look at Syl as he did.

Syl bounced on his toes, never taking his eyes off the pitcher's feet. So he saw the moment the Oriole lifted his foot — his front foot!

Syl took off like he'd been fired from a cannon. He heard the Orioles' infielders shouting, saw the second baseman rush to the bag and stand at the ready. He dropped into his slide then, thrusting his right leg out and bending his left leg beneath him. His toe touched the bag and he hopped up, breathing hard, to find the second baseman holding the ball.

Both Syl and the Oriole infielder turned to the umpire.

"Safe!" the man yelled.

"Yes!" Syl pumped his fist in a quick celebration and then looked for Mr. Teacy. If he'd expected the ballplayer to congratulate him, he was disappointed. One curt nod was all he got.

Syl pressed his lips together. *I'll get that guy to clap for me if it's the last thing I do this game!* he thought with determination.

17

Sylvester was so distracted by his thoughts that he didn't realize A.C. had boosted the ball above the first baseman's head until he heard the crowd yelling. The Oriole jumped up, nabbed the ball, and beat A.C. back to the base for the out.

It happened so fast that neither Syl nor Eddie had a chance to run. Unfortunately, they both died on base because Duane grounded out.

"Sorry, Eddie. Sorry, Syl," Duane muttered. "I hung you out to dry."

It was the top of the sixth inning and the

score read Orioles 6, Comets 2. That's how it read at the start of the bottom half, too. The home run slugger had gotten up again, but this time, he'd struck out.

The mood in the Comets' dugout was glum. They only had one more chance at bat to get four runs for a tie, five to win. There was no guarantee they'd even get one.

But they did. Burk, up first, socked a sizzling line drive in the hole between first and second, good for a double. Then Trent beat the throw to first on a bloopered fly ball. Two men on, no outs. Steve singled, too, to load the bases.

Jim came up next, whirling his bat above his shoulder. He waited for the right pitch and, when it came, knocked a fly ball into right field. It should have been an easy out. But the outfielder muffed the catch! Burk and Trent both raced home, Steve stood up at third, and speedy Jim slid safely into second.

Two runs scored, two runners on base, and no outs! The Comets were on their feet, cheering and clapping for their teammates. Their cheers died a moment later when Eddie dribbled a grounder and was put out at first. They grew quieter still when Kirk became the second out.

"So, Sylvester, feel a home run coming on, by any chance?" Coach Corbin asked as Kirk trudged to the bench. His tone was light, but Syl could see hope in his eyes.

"I'll see what I can do," Syl replied from the on-deck circle. He approached the plate and readied himself for the pitch. He let the first two go by for balls, but he liked the third—a lot.

Pow!

The moment he connected he was sure

he'd hit a home run. He began his slow jog toward first base, admiring his hit. But then his admiration turned to horror. The ball dropped inside the fence!

"What're you doing, Syl?" Trent shouted. "Run!"

Syl was already racing toward first.

"Keep going!" Rod yelled.

Syl rounded the bag and headed for second. It was close, but he slid in under the tag. Safe! Even better, Jim and Eddie made it, too, crossing home plate to tie the game!

Syl didn't celebrate, however. If he'd just run all out, he might have stretched his hit into a triple. At the very least, it would have been a stand-up double instead of such a close call. He was sure Mr. Teacy would have something to say about his not "giving it everything he had."

Sure enough, Mr. Teacy gave him an angry glare when he caught Syl looking at him. Then he shifted his gaze to the third baseman.

A slow smile crossed his face. He pointed from Syl to third base. With his hands, he made a sliding motion, rubbing one onto the other.

Syl nodded his understanding.

Don't worry, I'll slide! he thought.

But Mr. Teacy wasn't finished communicating with him. Now he lifted one of his feet so that the metal spikes of his shoes shone in the sunlight. He touched one of the sharp points and made the sliding motion again, only this time, the gesture ended with his fingertips stabbing toward the third baseman.

Syl gawked in disbelief. *He wants me to spike the Orioles' slugger when I slide into third!*

18

Sylvester had intentionally hurt only one other player in his life. Back when he'd been listening to Cheeko's advice, he'd jabbed a second baseman in the ribs hard enough to make the boy gasp in pain.

It was an unsportsmanlike move, one that he'd regretted. In fact, he'd felt so bad about it, he swore he'd never do something like it again.

Yet here was Mr. Teacy ordering him to do much worse to another kid!

Not a chance! Sylvester shook his head vehemently. Even though his own spikes

128

were just hard rubber, he knew they'd do some damage if they rammed into flesh.

Mr. Teacy's expression darkened. He stared daggers at Syl and repeated his gestures again.

Syl just looked away. *Signal all you want, Mr. Teacy,* he thought. *I'm not doing it. I don't care if it would help us win the game. It's a dirty play, and I won't do it.*

He turned his attention back to the game.

A.C. was at the plate. When the pitch came, it must have looked as big as a beach ball, because A.C. hit it squarely. He dropped his bat and tore up the dirt on his way to first base.

Syl, meanwhile, took off for third. He timed his slide perfectly and touched the bag a split second before the Orioles' baseman received the ball.

"Safe!" the umpire yelled.

The Comets' fans and players went crazy,

clapping and cheering. There may have been two outs, but the winning run was within their grasp!

Syl dusted off his pants, risking a glance at Mr. Teacy as he did. He gulped when he saw the man striding toward him, a furious look on his face.

"I warned you not to disobey my instructions," Mr. Teacy said.

Syl was about to retort when he realized something was happening on the field. The Orioles' coach decided it was time to replace his pitcher. It was a sound move; after all, the hurler had given up four runs in the inning. He may also have hoped that by halting the game to change pitchers, he would slow the Comets' momentum.

While the new pitcher jogged to the mound, the Oriole infielders threw the ball around the horn. The third baseman leaped for a high catch, but missed. Syl turned to watch him retrieve the ball from the dugout. He half-expected to see Mr. Teacy standing behind him, his usual glare etched on his face. Instead, he found himself face-to-face with Mr. Baruth!

All the anger and the sense of betrayal Syl had been feeling that day bubbled to the surface. He crossed his arms over his chest. "What are *you* doing here?" he muttered. "Come to coach your newest best buddy?"

Mr. Baruth didn't reply. Instead, he knelt down to tie a loose shoelace. At that same moment, the Oriole returned with the ball. He passed the man as if he didn't see him.

Syl tapped the player on the shoulder. "Aren't you going to say hello?" he said, crossing his arms again and jerking his head at Mr. Baruth.

The Oriole stared at Syl in confusion. "Uh, okay. Hello." Then he threw the ball to his shortstop.

Syl blinked. Slowly, he dropped his arms to his side. His mind was whirling. "Why isn't he talking to you?" he whispered.

"Why would he?" Mr. Baruth answered, standing up. "I don't know him and he doesn't know me."

"You don't? But I thought—"

"I know what you thought," Mr. Baruth cut in. He motioned for Syl to step away from the bag so they could talk in private. "And I know who put that thought in your head."

Syl nodded knowingly. "Mr. Teacy."

"No," Mr. Baruth said. "You put that thought into your own head. He just let you keep thinking it, because being mad at me got you to do what he wanted you to do." He smiled broadly. "Until a moment ago, that is. When you refused to spike that Oriole, Mr. Teacy knew you were done with him. So he left."

"Oh."

Mr. Baruth tipped his head to the side. "Are you disappointed he's gone?"

Syl thought for a moment. "Not really," he answered truthfully. "I learned a lot from him, but I didn't really like him. He kind of scared me, actually."

Mr. Baruth chuckled. "You weren't the first person to feel that way about him, Syl. Believe me!" He pointed to the field. "That new pitcher's just about warmed up. I better be going."

"Won't you stay until the game's over?" Syl begged. "I have so many questions!"

"Another time, Syl. Right now, you've got a run to score!"

Syl gulped. "I do? How? How am I going to score?"

Mr. Baruth shifted his gaze over Syl's shoulder. "There's the one who can answer that question. See you around."

Syl looked behind him to see Coach

Corbin approaching. "Listen up, Sylvester," the coach said in a low voice. "There's a way we can win this one now. But it all depends on you!"

With that, he outlined his plan in a whisper.

"So what do you think?" he finished. "Can you do it?"

Sylvester straightened his shoulders and nodded. "I'll give it my best shot, Coach."

19

The delayed double steal—that's what Coach Corbin wanted to try. Duane, at bat, was to pretend to bunt. At the same time, A.C., at first, was to steal. If and when the catcher committed to throwing A.C. out at second, Syl was to steal home.

It was a very tricky play, one that depended on pinpoint timing, incredible speed, and the ability of the offense to fool the defense. If it worked, Syl had a good chance of scoring the winning run. But there were many ways it could fail. A.C. could be thrown out at second. Duane could muff the fake bunt.

Syl could take off for home too soon. Or the defense could spot the play and shut it down before it even begins.

Getting the third and final out now wouldn't be the end of the world, of course. A tie game would simply lead to extra innings. That was why the coach had decided to try the play.

"Let's go for it," Syl told him.

The Orioles' pitcher finished warming up. The umpire called, "Play ball!" The Orioles got into ready stances.

And Sylvester's heart hammered so hard in his chest he thought it would burst.

Duane looked nervous, too. Syl hoped his friend would be able to do his part. He willed him to take deep breaths to calm down.

I should follow that advice myself, he thought, and promptly did so.

The Orioles' pitcher got the ball. He put

it behind his back, twirling it in his fingers, and leaned in to get the signals.

Duane held the bat above his shoulder, poised and ready. A.C. shuffled into the base path. Syl took a lead, too, trying not to be obvious as he did so.

The third baseman glanced at him but didn't change his position.

Syl risked another two steps away from the bag.

The pitcher nodded, straightened, and went into his windup. His front foot lifted off the turf.

Go, A.C.! Go! Syl's mind screamed.

A.C. did go, just as the pitcher released the ball. Duane rounded into his bunt, moving his body so it blocked the catcher's view just for an instant. The shouts from the Orioles' bench must have told the catcher what was happening, however, for the second the ball hit his glove he was on his feet and throwing to second.

Syl didn't wait a moment longer. He put his head down and ran. As his feet churned through the dirt, he imagined Mr. Teacy chasing him like a dog after a squirrel. Adrenaline shot through his veins and spurred him to go even faster. He hit the dirt for his slide into home at top speed.

Sand and tiny pebbles ground into his backside. He didn't even feel it. He was too focused on reaching home.

The catcher stood at the ready. Syl heard him yell, saw him move, and then—*pop!* The ball hit the catcher's glove just as Syl swept across the plate.

Syl lay still, breathing hard. Gritty dust filled his nose and mouth. He didn't care. His ears were straining to hear a single word.

And then he heard it.

"Safe!"

Duane gave a whoop and yanked Sylvester to his feet. "You did it! Final score, Comets seven, Orioles six!" he shouted.

"*We* did it!" Syl amended.

He pounded his friend on the back, grinning from ear to ear. A second later, he and Duane were surrounded by the rest of the Comets, all of whom were whooping and cheering. Out of the corner of his eye he saw the Orioles gather at their bench, their shoulders slumped.

He felt bad for them, but that's what happens. Sometimes you win, sometimes you lose.

"Hey, Syl," Trent called, "how about a little celebration at the ice cream parlor? My folks will drive us — and better yet, they'll pay!"

"Sounds great!" Syl returned. "Say, have you seen my glove? I thought I left it on the bench."

Trent spied it in the corner of the dugout. "Is that it over there?"

"That's it. Thanks," Syl said. "I'll be ready to go in a second. Meet you in the parking lot."

He hurried to the corner and retrieved his glove. When he picked it up, an envelope fluttered from inside its pocket.

"What the heck?" He straightened and looked around. "Does this belong to anybody?" But his teammates were still so busy celebrating, they didn't hear him. Syl saw that the envelope wasn't closed, so he lifted the flap to see what was inside.

What he found made him suck in his breath. It was a very old, sepia-toned photograph of two baseball players. They wore different uniforms but were examining a baseball bat together. Sylvester identified the man on the left immediately: it was Babe Ruth. He wasn't sure who the man on the right was. Then he looked closer and gave a small laugh.

The second man's ears stuck out quite prominently on either side of his head. Syl still didn't know his name — not his real name, anyway — but he would have known those ears anywhere. They belonged to Mr. Teacy.

Syl flipped the photograph over and saw that there was a short message written on it. "To replace the one that was lost," the note read. It wasn't signed.

Epilogue

Sylvester Coddmyer III didn't plan on showing the photograph to anyone. But the day after he stole home, he changed his mind.

That afternoon, he found a very special book about baseball history at the neighborhood yard sale. The stories were fascinating, but the pictures were what really captivated him.

As he paged through the volume, he saw countless images of Babe Ruth, along with other familiar figures. There was Eddie Cicotte standing with "Shoeless" Joe Jackson and the rest of the Black Sox players. Jackie

Robinson, the man who broke through baseball's color barrier, had a chapter all to himself, as did the Negro League. A photo of Mickey Mantle made him smile. Sprinkled among the biographies and game recaps were graphs comparing stats of one player to another and lists of all sorts, including one of the sport's longtime record holders.

One name appeared on that list more than once: Ty Cobb. Sylvester was interested to see that, among other things, Cobb had stolen home more often than any other professional player — over thirty-five times.

Intrigued, Sylvester flipped to the index to see if the book had more entries about Cobb. He found one labeled "Cobb versus Ruth." He turned to that page.

"No way!" he breathed. There, right smack in the middle of the text, was a copy of his photograph!

"Ty Cobb and Babe Ruth with bat," the photo's caption read. Syl stared at it for a long time and then shivered.

Ty Cobb. T. C. *Teacy!*

Just to be sure, he scanned the blurb on Ty Cobb, looking for similarities between the long-dead ballplayer and the man he knew as Mr. Teacy. They leaped out at him one after another.

"Known for his bunting." *Check,* Syl thought.

"Top batting average of all time." Syl remembered Mr. Teacy's insistence that hits were better than homers because they helped batting averages. *Check again,* he thought.

"From Georgia. Hated for spiking basemen during slides." *Check and check,* Syl thought as he recalled the man's slight accent, as well as his spike-high slides.

He closed the book then. He didn't need any more convincing that Mr. Teacy and Ty Cobb were one and the same person.

"Who'd ever believe me, though?" he said to himself. He knew the answer, of course. And as if he'd conjured up the person just by thinking about him, the boy suddenly popped up from behind a table laden with glassware.

Sylvester grinned. Tucking his new book under his arm, he called out, "Hey! Snooky! Wait up! I've got something to tell you that I just know you're going to want to hear!"

Off Mike

A Memoir of Talk Radio
and Literary Life

Michael Krasny

STANFORD GENERAL BOOKS
An Imprint of Stanford University Press
Stanford, California

Stanford University Press
Stanford, California

Printed in the United States of America on acid-free, archival-quality paper

Library of Congress Cataloging-in-Publication Data
Krasny, Michael, 1944–
  Off mike : a memoir of talk radio and literary life / Michael Krasny.
    p. cm.
  ISBN 978-0-8047-5671-6 (cloth : alk. paper)
  1. Krasny, Michael, 1944- 2. Radio broadcasters--United States--Biography. 3. College teachers--United States--Biography. 4. Authors--20th century--Anecdotes. I. Title.

PN1991.4.K63A3 2008
384.54092--dc22
[B]

                              2007018732

Designed by Bruce Lundquist
Typeset at Stanford University Press in 11/15 Bell MT

Contents

Photo sections follow pages 98 and 206

Acknowledgments

A NUMBER OF FRIENDS, my sister, my wife, and my
daughters were kind enough to read this manuscript
in various stages of dress and undress and to comment with often
worthwhile and useful reactions and suggestions. For that generosity I
want to thank Kent Gershengorn, Eliot Rich, Nikki Meredith, Manfred
Wolf, Eric Solomon, Walter Bode, Geoff Green, Gerald Nachman, Bob
Goldberg, Les Marks, Adam Hochschild, Jeff Klein, Lillian Rubin, Mary
Lamia, Julian Greenspun, Lois Weissberg, and Leslie, Lauren, and Alexa
Krasny. I want also to thank Claude and Louise Rosenberg for their
generosity and Sydney Goldstein, Raul Ramirez and JoAnne Wallace
for their support. I owe a debt as well to all of my radio producers and
interns and especially to Robin Gianattassio-Malle and Holly Kernan
who have been unstintingly supportive of this book. I am grateful to
Alan Harvey and the exceptional staff at Stanford University Press.
My deepest and most profound thanks are extended here to my agent,
Amy Rennert, for her unshakeable steadfastness; to Susan Wels for her
brilliant editorial assistance; and to my wife, Leslie Tilzer Krasny, for
too many reasons to cite.

Off Mike